DEEP OVERSTOCK

#25: Soups & Stews
January 2025

> Soup is just a way of screwing you out of a meal.

Jay Leno

COOK - SOUPS/STEWS

Editorial

Editors-In-Chief: Mickey Collins & Robert Eversmann

Soups & Stews Editor: Robert Eversmann

Managing Editor: Z.B. Wagman

Poetry: Timothy Arliss OBrien, Jihye Shin & Nicholas Yandell

Prose: Robert Eversmann

Additional Copyediting: Sarah Denison

Cover: Louis Dalrymple. *Who Is in the Soup Now, from Puck*, 1889. The Art Institute of Chicago.

Contact: editors@deepoverstock.com
deepoverstock.com

ON THE SHELVES

7   Soup Recipe for Sharing with Roommates by Alina Kroll

11 How to Make Miso Soup (The Hero's Journey) by Frank Gallivan

12 LOVE-MADE SOUP by Susan P. Blevins

13 Bean and Ham Soup by Lynette G. Esposito

14 Japanese Soup by Rachel Turney

15 Soup Story by Julian T Stites

18 For the Missing Ones by Colette Tennant

19 First Sunday in September by Joan Mazza

20 Goulash by Marianne Taylor

22 A Short Album About Love by Salena Casha

26 When all is cold by Diana Raab

27 OATMEAL POEM by Janet McCann

28 Curried Peanut Soup by John Davis

29 The Ramen Shop by Nicholas Yandell

41 STEW by Susan P. Blevins

42 God's Soup by Lynette G. Esposito

43 Moving In by Joan Mazza

44 Italian Pasta (Sedani rigati) Soup Pan by Roger Camp

45 THE SOUP I INHERITED by Elizabeth (Betty) Reed

48 This is My Brain by Karla Linn Merrifield

49 PLUM SOUP by Janet McCann

51 Abundance by Joan Mazza

52 EWOK VILLAGE by Emily

58 Psychic Soup by Lynette G. Esposito

Letter from the Editors

Dear Readers,

Thank you for picking up the latest issue of *Deep Overstock*. We hope that these pieces will sufficiently warm you up on cold winter nights.

In this appropriately-appetizer-sized issue about soups and stews, we have a multitude of ingredients supplied by you. We have recipes, as well as art, poems and short stories all about how soups can fill you up and make you feel good, or not.

But don't fill up just yet! Our next issue is sure to be even more appetizing as our editors have picked some of their favorite past themes for *Staff Picks*. Please send us your pieces for any of the following themes: Fairy Tales, Paranormal Romance, Dreams, Horror, Structures, Animals, Beekeeping, Hacking, or Classics by February 28th!

Your grateful cooks,

Deep Overstock Editors

Soup Recipe for Sharing with Roommates
by Alina Kroll

  You'll have to start in the spring. Don't ask me why, ask the green onions why they shoot up with the sun streaming through my bedroom window. Ask the chickens my mother raises why they rest in their coop all winter, meat growing tender with each passing month. Ask the food bank down the road why it gives out buckets of carrots and potatoes all spring long. This recipe is best for the spring: light and full of color.

Ingredients:

1. The bones of one chicken
2. The meat of one chicken, preferably white, shredded
3. Green onions, one handful, cut into ¼ inch pieces
4. Carrots, as many as you like, cut into ½ inch pieces
5. Golden potatoes, about 4, cut into ½ inch pieces
6. Optional: one can garbanzo beans
7. One yellow onion
8. Garlic, a lot, minced
9. Spices
10. Olive oil, enough to cover the bottom of your pot
11. Water, approximately 5 cups
12. Red grapes, one bag

Recipe:

  Start making the soup two or three hours before you might be hungry. Be prepared for your roommates to wander in and out of the kitchen the entire time. They will ask how your day went and you'll tell them how your mother will not stop calling you. She leaves long voicemails inquiring about every detail of your life- how your classes are going, if you ate dinner, what you ate for dinner, if you've made friends, if you've finally gotten a job or not. You resolve to call her back on the walk home from class, but by the time class is over, you're already home chopping onions. You'll call tomorrow.

One of your roommates will ask "Is dinner ready?" at least five times. Wash the grapes; set them out for her. She will pretend not to notice, but she will stuff them in her mouth like a greedy raccoon when your back is turned. You used to ask if she was hungry, but now you just offer food.

Now that she's been placated, you can start the soup. First, open the bagged chicken carcass your mother stuffed in your backpack when you visited her this weekend. You saw her do it this time, but she has slipped food in without you noticing before, forgotten to tell you. There was a horrible moment in statistics when you reached for a binder and an unknown bag tumbled out in class. It ripped, spilling carrot and bones and who knows what else between desks. The smell lingered in the classroom for days. You sat in the back of the room for the rest of the semester.

Separate the meat from bones. Try not to grimace at the feeling of oily meat squishing between your fingers, cartilage sliding itself beneath your nails. Hear your mother's voice: "*Samira, it's just food. Be grateful. Don't make that face.*"

Separate the dark meat from white meat if you'd like. Prepare your broth by boiling the bones, cartilage, and any discarded meat in a medium pot[1]. If you have vegetable scraps, let them soften in the pot. The hot water will draw out their nutrients and flavor. Let the mixture cook until the water has turned oily and opaque. Strain the liquid into a large pot. The remains have no use except for the trash or compost.

Here is a trick: grate your onion. Chopping them makes the fumes go everywhere and irritates your eyes, and produces

---

[1] *I forgot to mention, but you need two pots for this soup. At least, you should use two. One for bones and scraps, one to saute onions and garlic in oil while you wait. If you are patient, you can just use one. But I am not, so I use two.*

relatively large chunks. Grating on them largely reduces the potential for crying over onions. It turns onions into a mixture of pulp and liquid which will saute perfectly, and won't be chunky in your soup.

When the onions are translucent, add garlic. Cook until fragrant, then add spices. My spice tin is a reminder of my grandmother, a replica of her metal spice box, purchased by her on a rare trip to India. It holds nearly every spice I use in this soup, but you might not have the same spices. It doesn't particularly matter what type of spices you use so long as you use plenty and their flavors go together.

Here are my favorites:

1. Cumin seeds - flavorful, deep, slightly nutty and spicy
2. Merchu - an Indian spice that is somewhat similar to chili powder. What's the point in making soup if it won't burn your throat on the way down?
3. Cholula hot sauce - not exactly a spice, but necessary to achieving optimal spiciness
4. Giru - an Indian spice with a light but complex flavor. Adds a delicious scent and flavor to cooked food.
5. Salt
6. Tumeric - a bright orange-yellow Indian spice. Slightly acidic or bitter taste, but great health benefits. Makes food a bright, inviting color. Warning: will stain clothing and counters!
7. Ketchup - another not-spice, but it's a great way to soften the turmeric's sharpness and add more complexity to the soup. You only need a few tablespoons.

Season liberally. Add the potatoes and let cook until almost tender. They take much longer than carrots to soften. Then, add carrots, any other vegetables you might want, and the chicken. Cook until tender. Save the green onions for toppings- you don't want them to wilt and lose their bright color and crunch.

Yell "Soup's ready!" if your roommates haven't already smelled the soup and wandered into the kitchen. Ladle it into big, wide bowls. Let your roommates sprinkle on extra green onions. Text your mother a picture of the soup and dial her number.

How to Make Miso Soup (The Hero's Journey)
by Frank Gallivan

Gliding open that storied steel door
with foraging eyes

I meet the usual suspects
sitting listless in cracked tupperware

sleeping in creased beeswax
wraps stacked like rubble

and I sigh deeply
then turn away

and regroup–
mustering the courage
to look once more

to tread the dreaded boundary
between routine and imagination

to fight or to flee
suspended in midair
and the ticking of clocks

until I remember the dashi
and miso lingering in the back

and the path opens up
just a crack

and the fragments of me
reassemble

and I swing that storied steel door open
with a hero's chin.

LOVE-MADE SOUP
by Susan P. Blevins

So much more than chicken and vegetables,
your kitchen, your chopping,
watching, stirring.
What about your life experience?
It all goes in the pot you bring me
to heal my illness and cheer my spirits.

You bring me love-made soup with all
life's ingredients, covering all bases.
And body and soul respond!
It's all in the intention.
The recipe requires we simmer it first,
measure our life in tidy sips, then
bring to the boil of passion and
cook until done.

A whole new meaning to 'love-making'

Bean and Ham Soup
by Lynette G. Esposito

I sat at the kitchen counter
of my dad's gas
station
while he cooked
lima bean and ham soup.
I hated it.

What makes a poor child
so arrogant she could hate
her own dad's soup
then sit and eat as if
it were chocolate
because he made it for her.

Japanese Soup
by Rachel Turney

Soup Story
by Julian T Stites

It had a mind of its own. I served it to people and it killed them. Let me explain. Long ago, when I was a boy, my father made a special soup to serve people. It was an instant success. He called it "the magical soup" and would never share the recipe with me or anyone else. My father was a very secretive man. There were many things I didn't know about my father, but I digress. He was a chef, not just a chef, but a world renowned chef at that. He had restaurants all over the country, yet for as renowned as he was, he only served soup and wine at his restaurants. People came from all around to eat at his restaurants and try his magical soup. I was probably the only person in the world who hadn't tried his soup and I never intended to. Little did I know that would change.

I noticed that when people ate my father's soup, they would go into a trance-like state and often do weird things. Sometimes even wild or evil things. In all honesty, I feared my father and his magical soup. One day after being away at college, I came home to find my father slumped down dead in his favorite recliner, a bowl of his magical soup sitting next to him on the side table with the spoon still in the bowl. Looking down, I saw a pistol in his hand! The side of my father's head was bloody and there was a hole where his left ear had been. I screamed my head off. After calling the police and the paramedics, I sat down in my chair and wept. The police arrived moments later. After reviewing the scene, they ruled it a suicide and left me to collect my myself, as they sat there and wrote their reports.

Later that night I stood by the chair where my father had died and cursed. I wept until I fell asleep, waking up hours later. Then I saw it! A piece of ragged and tattered paper sitting beside the bowl of soup, and a letter addressed to me. I read the letter three or four times in disbelief, for on the old tattered and worn piece of paper was an ancient recipe, the ingredients to my father's magical soup and how to make it. The recipe and its contents were revolting. My father made it clear that I had no choice; the soup must continue to be made, and people must eat it. Now I stand in my restaurant, a gift from my long dead father. I ladle the soup into bowls by the dozen, and watch in anger and horror as the people blindly gobble it up, slowly losing their minds and their souls. The soup tried for years to get me to eat it, but I wouldn't. I wouldn't do it. The thought was repulsive to me. I knew I could never tell anyone what was in the soup, nor could I tell how it was made. I had never had any children and I planned on having the letter and the recipe buried with me when I died.

Suddenly I heard a beeping and I looked up! There was a blinding bright light and I heard a voice say to me that I was alright, that I was safe. Sitting up in the bed, I saw the nurse talking to me. It's time for breakfast, I looked in horror as she tried to force feed me the soup! I recoiled and shook violently. She had some orderlies come in and tie me down to the bed. I struggled with all my might, but there was nothing I could do! She sang to me as she spoon fed me, laughing at the glazed look in my eyes. "Everything is alright now young man, you're safe now."

I felt the soup flow through my veins and to my surprise, I felt very calm. My anxiety was dissipating, and for the first time in a long time, I could think clearly. "Wha-what did you do to me," I asked the nurse?

"I gave you your medicine. You have been in a severe psychotic episode for the last few days and have been refusing your medication. You started rambling about a bowl of soup and its recipe, killing people and making them into zombies."

I shook my head back and forth in an effort to clear the remaining cobwebs. I sat there pondering the words she had spoken to me, slowly digesting them. For some reason, what she said made sense. I laughed, feeling quite relieved! My heart was filled with joy. After a while, they unstrapped me from the bed and let me walk around the ward. I even played a game with a peer and worked on a puzzle, feeling the best I had felt in a long time. Breakfast came and went, and the day passed by quickly. They had given me my afternoon meds and I was feeling really good. Soon it was time for dinner and I lined up with the rest of my peers.

When I approached the window, my joy turned to horror! They were serving soup! The soup I had grown to loathe and hate! "Here you go love, have a bowl of soup and a nice piece of pie to go with it," the lunch lady said to me. The screams echoed from my mouth, and I fainted. I woke up hours later strapped yet again to a bed and this time, I saw a police officer standing in the corner of the room.

"He's awake," the cop told the doctor, who had walked in the room.

"Why did you attack the lunch lady, Justin?" The doctor asked.

"She tried to give me the soup! The soup that kills, the soup that is evil!"

The doctor shook his head sadly. "I was afraid you'd say that Justin."

"He knows," the cop said." We have to do something." Suddenly the doctor walked over to me and I felt a needle in my arm and I passed out. The next thing I knew, I was ladling soup in the restaurant that my father had left me and people were laughing and eating and I was once again calm. "The patient is under control once more," a voice said."He is doing what we have programmed him to do. We will continue the experiment and the study."

"Will he ever realize he is schizophrenic and that we are trying to help him?"

"Shut up and eat your soup," the voice said, laughing a coarse and evil laugh.

17

For the Missing Ones
by Colette Tennant

I need recipes for exotic dishes –
things they never dreamed of in
my ancestors' hometown of Fly, Ohio.

What about Lost Sister Soup –
some strange mixture of bone broth,
spring greens, mushrooms
foraged in faraway hills,
and salt pure as baby's blood?

I want a meat pie, its filling
the color of Phoenix feathers,
crust the color of a desert – one
where travelers never get thirsty
or lose their way in the night.

How about chocolate cake,
icing thick with
a Trinity of Spices?
I hope it's true – one taste
cures any heartache.

First Sunday in September
by Joan Mazza

A toasted English muffin with egg salad
with the crunch of organic celery.
Radio— songs from the sixties, ballads
with lyrics I learned better than any
memorized theorem for Regents exams
in high school. I sing along between bites.
Lunch is a rack of ribs from a lamb,
artichoke stuffed with seasoned breadcrumbs tight
between the prickly leaves. Two homemade soups
simmer on this chilly day, both bean and lentil,
make this house a home. Near the door, rain boots.
Nowhere to go, I'm experimental,
no longer need to be chief worrier,
taking tours of my dark interior.

Goulash
by Marianne Taylor

Coming home from playing in the snow,
handmade mittens soggy, smelling
like sheep, toes frozen from snow
that slipped inside too loose boots,
steamed up windows signaled serious
cooking afoot. And the aroma, vegetal
yet grounded in earthy beefiness,
my Grandma's goulash, quite the dish.

Onions, carrots, potatoes, tomatoes
and braised stew meat, a cheap
cut that softened, melted with heat
and time. Top notes of garlic and yes,
paprika, the real deal from one of
the European stores in the old town
where once my grandparents lived.

I'd shop with Grandma for bryndza there,
that salty cheese to top halusky.
It too smelled like sheep, made of their
milk, and eversotasty on noodles drenched
in melted butter. We'd buy poppy seeds to
soak in honey for holiday bobalki and cakes.

She rolled the dough for pastries or pierogi
with strong strokes, just as she kneaded
and punched the bread dough we'd put to rise
beneath a featherbed to keep it warm.
I'd nap there too, in yeasty peace.

I'd dream that I was her, asleep in the hay
of her grandfather's barn, waking to cousins
at play, sure of their place under the sun,
the wide Carpathian Mountains, their home.

When I awoke, it was time to bake or cook
or savor the flavors she taught me to favor,

the heat, the salt, the buttery and sweet.

Now, in my kitchen she is near, her clear blue eyes, white hair. Her name is Anna. She knew

that food and home and love are all the same.

A Short Album About Love
by Salena Casha

For Marlene, soup was a broth, cataract cloudy, noodles skimming the surface like a net. It was the type she poured from packets bought at Star Market and mixed with dehydrated chicken bits and imitation carrot. Historic mushrooms wrinkled from their time out of ground set against gluey celery. Granular, no matter how hot the water, birthed from a gentle sanded silt that settled on the bottom. Sometimes, when she was desperate, she'd drink it straight from the paper carton, the cardboard giving way bit by bit until she found it when she was flossing, pulling shreds from between her teeth.

Mostly, she reserved the liquid for late winter nights when the snow closed her door off to the rest of the world and she'd heat the water frantically on the stove because she didn't own a kettle, hoping to get it hot enough before the power inevitably went out. Those days, she drank it fast and irregularly other days out of cracked teacups that her grandmother left her. It always burnt and left her gasping. Never full.

When she met Ben, it was fall. Coffee shop mix up: she'd picked up his latte and he, her americano, black. A fumbled exchange by the cardboard stirrers, both promising they hadn't drunk from the others' even though Marlene had. She held the foam in her mouth for a few moments before swallowing it down her esophagus. A salve of bubbles for future blisters; winter was coming.

I should try a latte sometime, she thought to herself, the immediate calculus of calories and cost held at bay, cordoned off from the present because she couldn't stop looking at his hands, the perfect half moon nails except for the thumb bitten to the quick, the way he held the cup around the sleeve. How it might hold her arm just below the sleeve.

Left-handed, she decided, until he shifted it into his right.

"Let me buy you one, as an apology," she said, and his eyes widened with his lips, a smile absorbed in a gentle laugh. "It's the least I can do because I did actually drink from yours."

They ended up sitting together before heading to work and, found themselves late and breathless, on each others' phones. Exchanging books. Music. Time.

"It's soup season," he wrote to her once and she was too new to him to disagree, to break the news that soup, for her, was for desperate times when darkness outweighed light and that, as she cradled her phone like something precious, this particular set of days felt less and less like a desperate time and more like the cracking birth of a summer.

"Maybe," she wrote back.

"Maybe?! Babe, it's after Halloween," he replied. "We'll make soup this weekend."

She lingered on the taste of *babe*, on the casual unfurling of *we*. Given her predilection to soups that took less than a few minutes, soups that had the sound of a microwave ting, of singed skin and imitation egg, she was suspicious. It felt as though she'd cracked the door to invite single-hood back into a space where it didn't belong. So, then and there, she vowed not to let her definition of soup mess things up for her this time.

"Sounds lovely," she wrote back. "Consider it a date."

Because, she hedged, they were still *considering* this sort of thing.

The weekend arrived, a spray of New England autumn snagged between the end of fall and beginning of winter. She shook off her superstitions and picked up a white wine, an unnamed Chardonnay, because that was what Instagram told her went well with chicken broth, and wrapped herself in a scarf twice her height before heading to his.

The smell outside his door was roasted butternut, the flesh crisped a deep pumpkin in the oven. There was pumpkin and cold cream and nutmeg and coriander. It made her think of lattes, the new fall flavors she'd begun to experiment with, spiced insides. The playlist was all *The Smiths* and *Divine Comedy* and *Leonard Cohen*, carving the night with hymnals of longing, of paths crossed in Waterloo Station. Mesmerizing narratives, love stories in disguise.

But maybe, she chided herself, she was just reading into it like she always did.

She sat at the small kitchen table with the unseasonal frosted wine glass as he wielded a handheld immersion blender and moved, like a dancer, from stovetop to sink. The timing, impeccable, everything rescued before burning or just as the clock counted down to five. There were no brewing bones, just vegetal flesh, and she wondered when she'd admit it: that she had never had soup that wasn't from a can, a packet, that wasn't freeze-dried for the survivalists.

That she'd never had a soup that someone else had made from scratch. For her.

It was too late to admit it when he set the bowl in front of her. Cerulean porcelain backlighting the amber, a combination she'd chosen for her childhood bedroom. She thanked him for the performance, and he thanked her for the company even though they hadn't said anything for fear of breaking the music's spell, and she dipped the spoon in like she'd seen in movies, tipping silver with gold wax.

She felt the heat before she tasted it, the way it opened a window in her chest. Her rib cage gave a peculiar crack, not a break per se, but more a dissolve of tendon, a letting go, of cartilage melted away to expose bone.

"I need to tell you something," she said when she was over halfway through, even though she didn't know how to name it: that feeling of wanting to live inside the warmth of his flatshare, to put that particular playlist in that particular order on repeat, and to eat nothing else for the rest of her life.

He smiled and set down the spoon and their eyes locked over the scarred wood of the third-hand table, his roommate's from their college dorm.

"It's really that bad?" he asked.

And she laughed, her stomach cramping with the richness.

"I've never had anything like this before," she said, finally.

"Are you talking about me? Or the soup?" he asked, quirking a sarcastic eyebrow at the soup.

"Both," she said, and he laughed.

"It's magic, so I'm not surprised," he said. And then, more seriously, reached across the table to grab her hand. "A secret ingredient I'll tell you about sometime if you're lucky."

They sat like that, the fumes of fall mixing in their hair and in their clothes, the steam twinning between their hands and Marlene knew she would never, ever be the same and when she went home that night, she tossed all the soup packets she kept in her pantry, the mushroom creams and the chicken noodles and the one-pot ramens away, once and for all.

When all is cold
by Diana Raab

Try to turn up the warmth:
the hot cup of tea, the adoring puppy,
the morning sun through your writing studio window,
the Rumi poems, your healing sauna,
your crispy chocolate chip cookies,
a recipe from your grandma,
and the matzo ball soup from
your long-gone aunt,
the bag of potato chips left unopened,
the pink bathrobe you got for Christmas,
your laptop and the thesaurus
holding all your new words
and the hot shower
that you begin and end your day with.

OATMEAL POEM
by Janet McCann

swirls of brown sugar, lumpy soup,
golden pools of butter.

no, you say, *no!*
not this!

the fireside, the cold walk to school.
have you got everything?

just gimme a granola bar.

the warm, sweet glue.
spooning it up. raisins.
sticky spoon, residue of gum
in the blue bowl.

look, not even the cat will eat it.

but I want you to swallow it all down,
my round window, the bed
plumped up, the afghan with green diamonds,
father at the gate,
Betty and Peter waiting
at the end of the gravel walk.

you used to eat this stuff,
were you poor?

to swallow the taste
of sweet melted cardboard,
I will give you my silver spoon
with the rolled handle.
a whiff of kerosene.

are you ready now?
it's time to go.

Curried Peanut Soup
by John Davis

Simmer peanut butter and honey. Hum
    the yum of flavors the way you hum her sway
in a black dress. Mince the onions

and garlic. Remember her smile
    as smooth as ginger when you sauté
and salt. You spin-in cinnamon.

How sweet her lips. Curry-in
    the turmeric. Spice the cayenne—alive
as the wet and wild you thrive with her.

Cardamon, cumin, cloves. Bulk them
    with buttermilk before you diagonally slice
bananas. Drizzle with lemon juice.

A pinch of cinnamon. How she pinches
    your places. How she corianders
your heart. Skillet the bananas

in peanut oil. Let them lose their shape.
    You lose your shape, become one shape
when the two of you simmer to a boil

and pour yourselves into a bowl.

The Ramen Shop
by Nicholas Yandell

The Ramen Shop was near closing when a young man walked in. Though 20 minutes before the posted time, Grace had never had a problem kicking people out early, or opening late for that matter. If anyone ever asked her about whether she lost customers for her erratic hours, she'd just say, "If they've had my ramen before, then they'll wait or they'll come back. If they've never had my ramen, and they miss their chance, then I pity their souls."

She had plenty of regulars, even though she never advertised, had no website or any kind of listing. She had never used a computer, or cell phone, and just had a landline for emergencies. She had a manual credit card machine, but all the regulars knew how she hated using it, so they always brought cash, or checks, or offered produce in trade.

The Ramen Shop was only given an actual name for tax purposes, and the sign, which had predated Grace, had been a gift to the previous owner from a local craftsman. The letters spelled the word "Ramen" and were made of hand-blown, green glass, illuminated by bulbs from within. The previous owner had never wanted or felt like she needed a sign, but appreciated the effort of the craftsman, so it found a home. Having such bright glowing letters had the mixed blessing of occasionally bringing in those who were not regulars, especially the "mountain tourists," made of mostly 20-something skiers and snowboarders. This young man who entered was most definitely a "mountain tourist."

It wasn't his snowboard boots that gave him away or any of his unusually colorful winter gear, but his head of long, sweaty, sun-bleached, blonde hair. Grace thought no ill will of the "mountain tourists," but she also didn't understand them, especially the way they stared at electronic devices all day. She was always polite, but generally made no further efforts to engage with them.

He was pulling off his gloves and hat as she made her way over. Though planning to gently kick him out, something about the sting of red on his cheeks and his somewhat pained expression changed her course.

"Good evening," she said. "May I get you something?"

He seemed unable to speak for a moment, but eventually choked out the words: "Umm. Tea or water maybe?"

She went about fixing his tea, happy that his request was at least an easy one. Tidying up as she waited for the water to heat, her eyes kept straying to his hunched over form. His coat and leg coverings were torn, and the redness on his face appeared to be a scratch of some type. She couldn't put her finger on it, but there was something desperate and maybe even tragic about him.

Had he been a regular, Grace would have immediately said something like: "You must have had a hard day. Would you like to tell me about it?" And he likely would have, because she was known to be an exceptional listener. Though curious, she didn't feel it proper to engage someone like him in this way.

When she finally brought him tea and a glass of water, the young man took them, nodded, and then gulped the water down with ferocity. When he picked up the still steeping hot tea, she worried he would do the same thing, and blurted out: "Be careful! It's quite hot!"

He seemed very startled, so Grace added, "I just didn't want you to burn yourself. Here, let me fill your water."

She quickly returned, poured him a glass, and left the pitcher with him. He gulped down two more waters, and was working on a third, when she said:

"I just wanted you to know that we'll be closing up soon. Is there anything else I can bring you?"

"Uh… no. Thank you. Or well, I guess, do you have a

bathroom?"

"Yes. It's through the kitchen. I'll show you."

As she led him into the back, he seemed to barely have the energy to even walk, and she was concerned that he might collapse. He closed the door and it was perhaps 10 minutes before he emerged. He then headed straight for his table, picked up the tea, drank it down, finished the pitcher of water, and then grabbed his stuff. He looked like he was about to just head out, but then stopped, turned around and said:

"I'm sorry. Um. How much do I owe you?"

"Oh. Don't fret. It's my treat."

"Uh. Okay. Thank you then."

Just like that, he was out the door and into the cold. She walked over to lock the door, but just as she got there, it opened and the young man popped his head in saying:

"Do you know where the bus station is?"

"It's just two blocks to your left, but I'm sorry to tell you that there are no more buses tonight. They stopped service because of the storm. This town has good plows though, so they'll be running by morning."

He looked devastated, but nodded and was just about to leave, when Grace asked:

"Are you staying somewhere close?"

He hesitated, then said:

"I don't have any place to stay. Do you know anywhere I could go to keep warm?"

She thought, *Looking like he does, with no place to go, on a night like this, poor thing!* Immediately, she said:

"Come in, please, and follow me."

As he entered, she noticed that his outer layers were soaked, and he was shivering. He followed her as she pulled out a chair and placed it near the fire.

"Take off all your wet clothes and hang them on the mantle; I'll go find something to put around you."

She headed back into the kitchen, retrieving a thick shawl she wrapped up in on nights like this when she slept overnight in the Ramen Shop. Returning, she was slightly shocked to see the young man standing there in front of the fire, wearing nothing but a pair of ripped purple underwear and a thin undershirt.

She hadn't realized quite how literally he would take what she was saying, but simply handed him the shawl. He wrapped it around his shivering body and sat near the fire. For someone quite fit and just under six feet tall, she thought he looked surprisingly fragile and delicate.

Heading back into the kitchen, she put the kettle on for more tea, and returned to him with the piping hot cup. The instant young man took the cup, he broke out in tears, which he tried to cover, and then finally spoke up. "Thank you so much. I don't even know your name, but you've been so kind to me and I'm just such a total mess that I can't even imagine what you think of me right now."

"Well, my name is Grace and just because one is a total mess, doesn't mean they shouldn't have a place to be warm, and have something warm to drink."

He smiled for the first time. "I'm Mason," he said. "Nice to meet you. Yeah, I guess what I meant is that 24 hours ago, I never could have imagined myself, stranded in this town, in this closed down shop, drinking tea, in my underwear, wrapped in your shawl. I'm thankful, but I think I'm also in shock after the day I've had."

"Well, we have no place to go until morning, I can refill your tea whenever you like, and we have this fire to keep us warm. Would you like to tell me about it?"

"Well, it's kind of a rough story, but I guess I can if you want."

"Yes, please continue."

"Well, last week everything started falling apart. First my boyfriend broke up with me and kicked me out. Then I was literally sleeping in the studio where I was supposed to record. I was a singer with a record contract, and was trying desperately to hold it together and give them what they wanted, but it was not going well. I guess I couldn't fake it anymore, and halfway through, the label let me go.

"At that point, I felt like I had nothing, and was nothing, and just didn't care anymore, so I took what little money I had and came up here to snowboard and clear my head. I just kept recklessly leaving the trails, not even thinking of the danger. When I accidentally found myself on the road instead of the lower runs of the park. I stuck out my thumb, and a guy picked me up in his truck.

"I was pretty blasted from pills at that point, and I blabbed on and on telling him all about how I was alone, had been riding isolated backtrails all day, and even told him my phone was dead when I asked him for a charger.

"After like an hour and a half, I finally realized that we must have passed the ski park. When I brought it up, he said:

" 'Oh. I guess we better find our way back then. I know an alternate route that'll get us there faster.'

"He turned onto this dirt road, where there were no houses around us. It started snowing, we went under this really dark canopy of trees, and just kept going up. Feeling uneasy at that point, I said: 'You sure this is taking us there?'

"At that, he said. 'You're right. I might need to check the map.'

"He stopped on a pull-off, right up to and almost touching this low metal railing. He pulled out a map, looked at it for a second, then rolled down his window and took a look outside.

He pulled his head back in, and then asked me:

" 'Hey, can you poke your head out, look around, and see if you see sign markers?'

"I was kind of annoyed that he didn't know where we were, but did what asked, and right as I got my head out, he yanked really hard on the back of my pants, and I hit the top of my head on the edge of the window. He dragged me in and in seconds, was on top of me. He was a few inches taller than me, outweighed me by at least a hundred pounds, and easily held me down. My pants were already halfway down my leg, he ripped my underwear, and I just remember cold air hitting areas of my bare skin that it was never supposed to come into contact with.

"The rest of what happened in the car is a blur, and I don't feel like pushing myself for more details. There was a point though, when he shoved my face into the cracks of his seat, and lit up by the cab light, I could see the contents underneath. There was a bag, a shovel, a hunting knife, and some kind of gun.

"Though I'd been recklessly risking my life the last few days, now faced with this terrible possibility of death, my survival instinct finally kicked in. I focused on some switches on the edge of the seat, managed to slip my hand down and pull one, and it collapsed my seat right on top of him. He must have slammed into the dash, because an alarm and flashers went off, and in the chaos, I managed to squeeze out from under him, pry the door lock open, crank the handle, and dump myself out of the door. I hadn't even thought about where we were though, and tumbled over that railing of what I guess was a bridge into some kind of deep ravine.

"This fall could have easily killed me, but a tree branch caught my coat. I managed to grab the side of the bridge and pull myself into this crevice underneath.

"I stayed completely still, lying on my stomach, in this tight, spidery crevice. As he turned off the alarm and lights, I was so terrified that he might hear me, that I didn't even try to pull my pants up and you can imagine how uncomfortable that was. He then came over to the edge and shined a flashlight down into the deep ravine. He probably saw the broken branches, but the crevice was concealed from his view. At that point, he probably realized that he shouldn't be seen anywhere close to where my body might be found, so he took my backpack and snowboard, threw them off the bridge, and took off.

"I laid there in that crevice for way too long, and I don't even know how I had the strength and will to pull myself up and over that bridge rail. I was terrified of staying on the road, worried that the guy might come back to check this spot, so instead, I found an unmarked hiking trail, followed it, and it somehow ended right across the street from you. I'd nearly resigned myself to death, when I saw the light of your 'Ramen' sign, and then realized I was going to live."

Grace was visibly struck by this final statement from Mason. He immediately noticed, got a little uncomfortable and since she wasn't saying anything, he mumbled out a response of:

"I'm sorry. I know that's probably revealing way more than you wanted to hear."

"No. On the contrary. I feel blessed that you felt comfortable telling me something so personal. I'm so sorry you had to go through that. Do you need medical help?"

"I don't think so. I checked myself over in your bathroom earlier, and I think I'm physically okay. What's really weird though, is that even after everything that's happened, I'm feeling a level of safety and calmness right now that I haven't felt since I was a kid."

"Hmm. Please, if you don't mind. Tell me about that. What was different for you back then when you were a child?"

"Well, for one thing, my father was alive back then. He knew how to make me feel safe, even as a gay kid growing up in a small town. He passed away when I was 15 though, and my mother had died before I had much of a memory. I was an only child, and didn't really have anyone else around to make me feel that safety. I never thought I'd have it again either. I figured I should just go out there and face my fears. Well, living fearlessly, became living recklessly, and I guess pushing everyone else away, so I could only rely on myself. Now, after barely surviving these three close calls, and knowing that I'm mostly responsible for bringing myself so near such harm, I feel almost guilty being presented with what you've offered me. This safety is so foreign, and I can't help feeling like I don't deserve it. I deserved to die in that car, or off that ledge or on that trail. That would have been the logical result of my life's choices, but instead I'm sitting here with you."

Mason was in tears at this point and wasn't even trying to hide it.

Grace put her hand on his shoulder and told him:

"This kind of safety you talk about, it's vital, and there's no reason to feel like you should be deprived of it."

"Sure, I get that. I guess I still just feel like such a mess and don't really know what I'm living for, that's what's hard."

At that point, Mason, absent-mindedly ran his hand across his thin torso, and noticing, Grace immediately said:

"You must be so hungry, let me make you some ramen."

"Sounds like a dream, but it's so late, and you've worked all day and already done so much, I can't possibly ask you to go make me food."

"Well I can't let you leave this place without offering you the finest gift I have. It won't take me long, and perhaps you can help me while I work. You see, my record player has been broken for weeks and I've been without music. Maybe you could sing something for me?"

"Really? I don't have a guitar or anything, so I don't know how good it's gonna sound, but if that's what you want, sure. I'll sing for some ramen!"

Heading into the kitchen, as Grace began cooking, Mason

started tapping out a rhythm with his hands on the counter. His voice, though it started out timid, quickly settled in. With Grace's encouragement, he sang the whole time the Ramen was being made. Songs of whimsical adventures, lost loves, hopeful futures, he even started making up one about the ramen shop. Listening to him, Grace was mesmerized, and felt terrible interrupting him when the Ramen was done.

They sat with their bowls in front of the fire, and the instant that first spoonful hit Mason's mouth, he said.

"Wow. This ramen is like magic or something! I don't know if it's just crazy late night delirium, but I feel like I'm seeing a life before me, that I'd never seen before. You know what I mean?"

"I certainly do."

"Oh yeah, speaking sort of on that subject, I wanted to ask you something?"

"Please do then."

"After I told you about my harrowing experience, and I talked about seeing your 'Ramen' sign, and what it meant to me, I noticed a reaction from you. Made me want to know about how you ended up here."

"Well, in many ways, this ramen shop saved my life as well. In my early 30s, I was diagnosed with what I thought was a terminal disease and I couldn't afford any of the offered treatments. I came to this town, because I had always found such peace on visits here and I thought of no other place I would rather die. I had assumed I would only live a matter of months, but upon first entering this town, I first saw this ramen shop. I walked in, had a bowl, started a conversation with the owner, and within an hour of meeting me, she offered me a job. By the end of the day, I had started something new, right when I thought everything else was ending."

"And how long ago was that?"

"30 years."

"Wow. So you survived an unexpected 3 decades?"

"Apparently, and I have no intention of going anywhere soon."

"Thank God for that. I understand why this place means so much to you then. That's so brave starting over like that. Did you have family or anything in that town you left behind, or any reason to go back?"

"No family. I had a few friends that I miss, but there was really only one major regret I have. I left behind someone who would've spent all of her money, and given up her dreams to try and save me, and I just couldn't have that though. I assumed my time was over, and I wanted her to live without my burden."

Seeing something new in her eyes. Mason immediately asked:

"Can you tell me more about her?"

"Well, her name was Elle Wallace. She was a fine musician like you. She had finally got a big break, as an opener on an international tour. It was her dream, and of course it happened right as I got my terrible news. I knew she would cancel her tour without a thought, and there was nothing I'd be able to do to talk her out of it. I did what I thought was best. I broke up with her and it did not go well. After she had left on tour though, overcome with regret, I left a letter at her place with papers showing my diagnosis and trying my best to explain why I truly had to leave. I have no idea if she ever received it. After surviving long enough to realize that my diagnosis was false, I was too afraid to reach out, figuring that she'd think I had lied about being terminal. I know it's silly to hold onto something like this for so long, but I still think of her far quite often, and wish things could have been different."

"You know, I bet she'd believe you if you two had the chance to talk."

"Oh, I wouldn't know how to find her, and I'm sure she has long moved on and forgotten about me, but thank you for allowing me to reminisce."

Their conversation continued into the early morning hours, until both of them fell asleep near the fire. Grace awoke and began preparing for the work day. Mason awoke shortly after to a strange yet newly hopeful existence. He put on his dry clothes, then they drank tea and had breakfast.

As it came near time for Mason's bus to leave, Grace said to him: "Spending the night with you was one of the most unexpected and delightful moments of my life. And to hear your voice and your songs! Please, go out there and share your talent. If you are able to create more music like what you showed me, you will move the world to tears."

"Wow. Thank you, Grace. You honestly helped me remember why I loved music in the first place, and so much more too. I can't possibly express how much your kindness has meant to me. You saved my life, and I'm serious about that. I will always remember you and your ramen!"

They hugged, said a few last words and then Grace, the Ramen Shop owner, watched Mason, the singer, walk away. She thought of him often over the next few weeks, especially when she was closing down the shop. It warmed her heart, remembering him singing for his ramen and she hoped to hear more of his music someday.

One evening, she'd sent her last customer away and was considering leaving early, when a person, bundled up in winter clothes came bustling through the door. For a split second, she thought maybe it was Mason, then put her eyes down, as she noticed the customer's feminine appearance. The person was taking her time approaching, so Grace figured she'd just finish her task before engaging.

Finally though, the woman moved up to the counter. Grace left the kitchen and when she neared the counter she looked up and said:

"May I help you."

"Grace?"

Taken aback, Grace stared at the woman, whose hood, hat, scarf, and coat were now removed.

"Elle… It can't be."

Tears formed in both of their eyes.

"Yes Grace. It's me. It's like a miracle seeing you in front of me."

"Yes, it is, but how on earth did you find me?"

"Well, I guess it all started when I was approached by a kind, exceptionally-talented, and very determined young singer named Mason. He told me he had been searching all over for me and when I asked him why, he said: 'because of Grace.' He then began talking nonstop about you, this little shop, and your ramen, which apparently has the power to make life worth living again."

STEW
by Susan P. Blevins

While outside it's raining, and sleeting and freezing,
inside my crockpot is bubbling with fragrant stew,
offering me generous comfort and companionship,
embracing the entire house with its delicious aroma of
tasty promise, a guarantee of sorts against the
cold and hunger,
hunger for food to comfort my body,
hunger for food to feed my soul with
culinary love and friendship.
Oh the good fortune that blesses me
with appreciation for the simple joys of life,
for nourishing food, and most of all,
for dear friends.

God's Soup
by Lynette G. Esposito

The stew splashed
as the wind stirred
the lightning-warmed
broth…
such a sight to see
at the beginning.

The new cook in the kitchen
took a sip and grinned…
This is good.

Moving In
by Joan Mazza

At last, more space to spread out and organize,
clear shelves and drawers to show what's inside.
Although I've resisted this extravagance, I've
given in so that I have space to freeze packaged
homemade soups, banana bread, and challah.

I'm not questioning this urge to have more
cooked food at hand, even if the new freezer
lives in the garage, one floor below my kitchen.
It's backup because I'm a child of fearful parents
who grew up during the Depression, who knew

what it was like to be hungry in every way
you'd use the word. A hurricane is churning
south of here, but a generator will keep me
running from fridge to freezer, moving clear
containers of minestrone, barbeque chicken,

veggies, chocolate cheesecake, chicken soup.
Tripling my freezer space, this new appliance
is ready for a cooking frenzy as I prep for
an apocalypse I won't live to see. Food:
another inheritance I'll leave for others.

Italian Pasta (Sedani rigati) Soup Pan
by Roger Camp

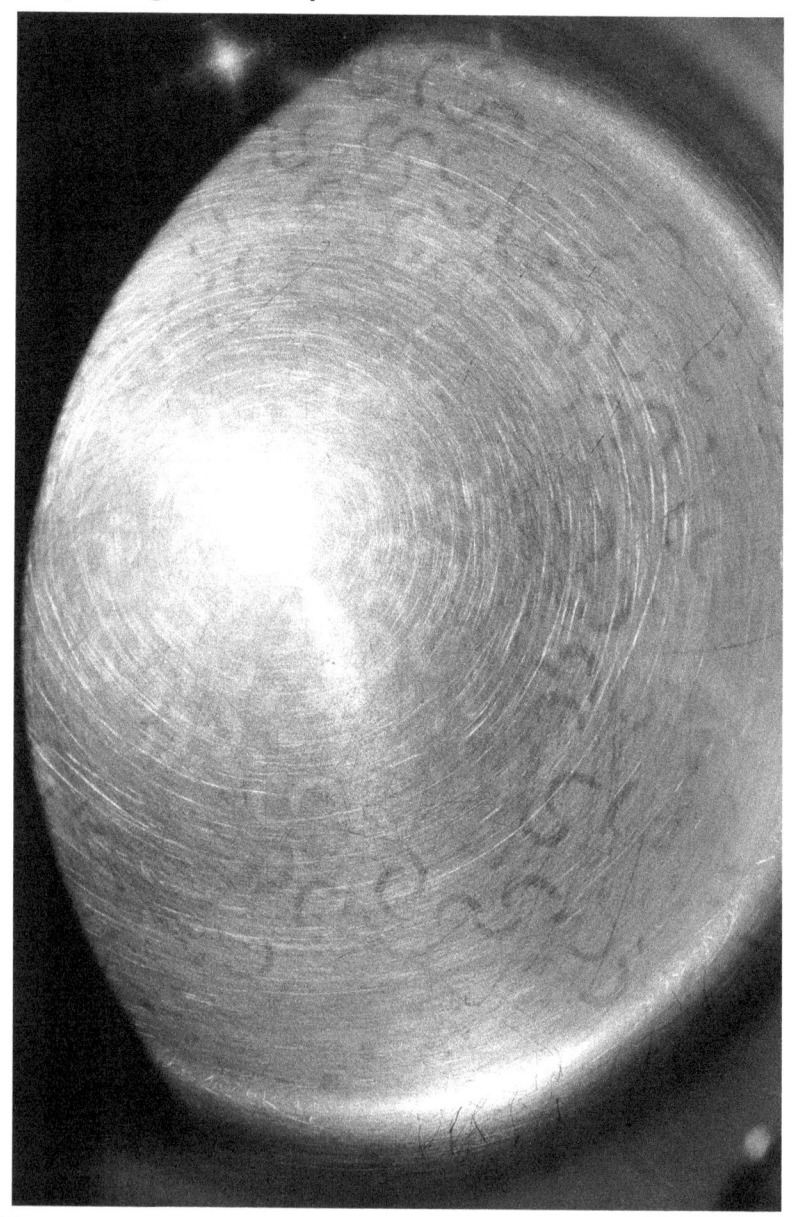

THE SOUP I INHERITED
by Elizabeth (Betty) Reed

I pick up the purple turnip and slice off the scraggly-rooted bottom so it is stable when I cut it in half. I haven't bought a rutabaga since the first heatwave in June. But the autumn chill compels me to buy this hybrid cabbage-turnip that I use only for soup. The ritual of peeling and slicing embodies Portuguese traditions passed down from one generation of women to the next. Like my great-grandmothers I make red kidney bean, chickpea, and cannellini bean soups with kale, spinach or savoy cabbage, adding a cup of ditalini, mini-elbows, egg pastina or rice.

I remove the thin, crackly skin of a tennis-ball-sized onion, a vegetable that draws on my emotions, spewing tears from my eyes before I've even cut it. Did my great-grandmother, exiled from her village to Lisbon to work as a cook for a wealthy family, cry when chopping onions? Did she think about the man, married, but not to her, who wrote her into an old story of impulse and impossibilities that ended with a child in her womb? The man who fathered four children, never with the same woman, never with his wife. The man who became the poster child of desire and freedom, while his lover became the poster child of shame, displacing my great-grandmother from her village, her family, her friends, the only world she knew. Her disgrace generated a new recipe of surveillance and rigid social restrictions for her daughter, my seamstress grandmother.

I peel the carrots and wonder if my grandmother blushed at their naked state, astonished that her mother and three unofficial aunts peeled off layers of village voices and Catholic chains to lie naked with a man who had nothing to lose? Did she wish she could peel the illegitimacy off her body, her name, her life? Did she long for the two half-brothers and one half-sister who shared the same father but sprouted from four women who remained untouchably single after giving birth? I don't know how long my grandmother hid her secret from the three daughters she gave birth to. She laid out and cut social straitjackets that laced up tightly, determined to end the stigma of illegitimacy. She stitched her daughters into antiquated patterns, accompanied everywhere by my grandfather. Three daughters who never dared to design a life outside of their parents' expectations and held their breath as my grandmother pressed them into the wedding gowns she sewed.

    I disrobe the garlic of its translucent ivory skin, like the wedding veil my grandmother created, laced with love, duty, and the satisfied success of marrying her third daughter without a taint of trespass, without the secret stain she lived with and that I only heard about in secret whispers from my cousins. A stain that embedded its tarnished core in my parents' chain of commandments for their own three daughters. No rides from anyone but them in high school. Chaperoned dating in college (in 1975.) No living on campus. But I credit them for supporting education, something my mother, who earned a full music scholarship to Oberlin college, erased from her life. There was no question of living so far away on a college campus, unleashed and unsupervised. Instead she worked at the Singer factory with my grandfather during the day and attended night school to earn her music diploma. I, too, lived at home through college, through two degrees in piano performance. And if I had obeyed their oppressive orders, orders that I bent, broke, cut and threw away, I would have lived at home until I married at the age of thirty-six.

    My mother stopped soaking the beans overnight, changing the water several times, and cooking them for an hour before starting the soup. The pressure cooker, her shortcut, cooked the beans in twenty minutes. The can opener is my shortcut, like the shortcut I took to my boyfriend's dorm room when I was supposed to be in class. The shortcut I took to my own apartment at the age of twenty-six ended the myth of waiting at home for my prince to show up with a ring and a promise. The shortcut I took on a plane to travel with a man I loved reintroduced shame into my parents' lives, but not mine. Shame slid off my shoulders. The shortcut that moved me into another apartment to live in sin for three years with my now-husband poisoned their recipe of rules with disgrace.

My daughter's girlfriend is the cook in their home. They requested the recipe for the red kidney bean soup. They ask me the same questions I asked my mother. What size pot? Why are there no amounts on the recipe card? How long does everything simmer? I write down what I can: an onion, a wooden spoonful of olive oil and salt, three celery stalks, half of a purple turnip, a garlic clove, a can of red kidney beans, a bag of spinach, a cup of egg pastina. But I know the real recipe lies in a box of women's constrained lives, a recipe of intangible ingredients that each generation now has the option to rewrite. It's a recipe I'm proud to hand down.

This is My Brain
by Karla Linn Merrifield

Unborn hole empties church
railroad ties in a forest
crawdads tadpoles nymphs sold out
who dreamed up Jupiter's moonscapes

Kelp and kale prom dresses
the hunter who bags his pal
no mention of French *parfum*
stenches of ghetto gutters

F-only alphabet soup de jour
minesweeper memories of fiscal statistics
but last place in *Ulsysses*
found living moodquick-change artist

born whole
my brain on my mind

PLUM SOUP
by Janet McCann

Boiled in the small pot
until they disintegrated. Now
a bubbling whirlpool of purple, tiny strings.
Pink roses rise to the surface.

A dish for a baby girl shower?
I dip—sweet, tart.
A ladle in Japan
spooning it over brown garlicky meat?

Such viscous roses! I dip out the pits
with a slotted spoon.
The roses break up, re-form.

How long will we cook over stoves,
watch the long loop of purple sauce
drip back to the resurfacing rose,
taste from the spoon, try to guess at
the deep foreign tang hidden in the fruit?

How long over the stove,
Mostly women but some men, stirring?

***

If everything were very nice, under
a kindly communist God, we each would
get to be eighty, then finis. A spouse
and two children. We are all only
slightly different. No need for doctors,
we are all healthy. Or dentists.
No crime, we all have the same things,
and over the years have grown less covetous.
Why would you want what you already have?

If everything were very nice, gardens would
be beautiful, some would make them their lives.

Others would sing or dance, few would choose words
because the stories are so much the same—
There are the births, those passionate events
and tiny cherished differences, but still... For lunch
you type in your request, the machine presents it.
Ribs with plum sauce? Check. Transparent soup?
Right here. No mess, no errors and no problems.

At eighty, on the bright appointed morning
We'd simply fade to outlines and then vanish.
If only everything were very nice.

***

It is done now, dark and thick and fragrant,
bubbles rise, translucent violet.
The scent of plum fills the house,
drifts out over the summer garden
like a haiku.

Abundance
by Joan Mazza

Now that I'm rich, I buy broccoli rabe by the bunch,
no matter what the price. Same for escarole, Swiss
chard, organic spinach, avocadoes, artichokes.

My grandmother pored through the bin
of discarded vegetables, haggled to get them
free, picked off decomposing leaves, and cooked.
Would she celebrate that I still prepare the foods

of her peasant origins: pasta *fagioli*, minestrone,
lentils, beans of every kind? I can buy anything
I want, happy I don't want a yacht or mansion

or a trip around the world. I live amid abundant
trees and flowers, redbuds and dogwoods blooming,
a pantry stocked for snow, rain, hurricanes, floods
of introversion. Birds delight in my offerings

of occasional pecans, *pignoli*, and macadamia nuts.
When I imagined wealth, I thought I'd have
flowers delivered daily, hire a driver so I could
sleep and be delivered to my destination.

Call me nuts. I'm not really rich, but feel flush
enough to share with others, make small donations,
never feel I'm wanting for anything I want.

EWOK VILLAGE
by Emily

What is time, and what is it made of?

Butter? Water? Sand?

No matter. It doesn't matter really. What was then is also now, and not just in my brain where timelines like to blend together and make my world confusing, but in actuality, too, if you believe in certain theories.

There are only two things that have ever made sense to me about time. One is the part of Einstein's theory of special relativity that came to him as he rode away from a famous medieval cuckoo clocktower in Switzerland and had the thought that every moment goes on forever depending how far out into space you go. Time is contingent on space, and if the universe is infinite, then so are all moments, too. Nietzsche said kind of the same thing with his doctrine of eternal recurrence, which is basically the idea that time is an infinite circle.

The only other thing that's ever made sense to me re: time is when my friend Elena said that time was just a big pot of soup.

◯

That being said, 9 years ago and also right now in my mind and forever some faraway point out in space/soup, Bill, Pete, and I are walking down the farm path to Ewok Village, lined with paper bag luminaria of candles and sand I placed there earlier today, the day of the harvest party at the farm where I live. It's late night. Behind us we can hear the party in the open-air toolshed growing quieter and quieter. Their band just finished playing and the whisky someone placed on a haybale for them is making the lights soften and glow. Pete is having a moment. He says this is exactly like a dream he's had many times, walking into the woods on a pathway of glowing lanterns, and he can't believe that it's just become real. And maybe that's what the farm and this summer is, a dream. Dreamtime.

Not a dream only in that dreams are blending into reality, but also like in dreams how things happen one right after the other and you can't always remember how you got from one place to the next.

You know the saying, "you only get so many summers?" This feels truer every year, and what also feels true is you only get so many truly memorable summers. This being one of them, it's hard to know what to say exactly. Certain times are just hard to distill, especially when what remains are mostly bursts of images and feeling like the temperature of a horse's breath on your cold morning hands, the smell of fermented vegetables and hog fire, the having left an entire life behind and then gone and lived amongst chickens who torment you each morning, and the kind of bursting embryonic feeling of growing vegetables while unraveling on the inside and out of that unraveling coming funny little songs that you sing to yourself alone in the fields. To tell of times like this is more like to pull a dusty patchwork quilt out of a closet and wrap someone with it so that they can smell and feel it, and then maybe nod off a little bit and go into a little dream.

Think of summer. Think of a farm. Think of a time your heart has fallen apart like an old hunk of bread. Think of a tiny flower sprouting out of it anyways. Think of heat. Like the incubation of an egg. Think of an egg cracking. Think of your hands in wet dirt and early morning. Think of garlic scapes, the curly stalks that grow out of the bulbs, and what your hands might smell like after gathering them. Think of poppy flowers in a big row next to a pile of rocks. (One of the kids visiting the horse camp saying "I didn't know they grew rocks here!") Think of an old wood-paneled station wagon left in the sun and how warm it would be to get inside it. Think of yourself speeding around the hairpin turns to and away from the farm/city as the winds of your life change direction and your thoughts whoosh in/out the open windows, curling into the smoke of the Pall Mall you shouldn't be smoking but do…just for now, just for today. (Do you know smoke moves exactly like water, only not beholden to the laws of gravity?) Think of a pink woven hammock in a quiet clearing in the woods next to, but away from all of this. Think of walking to it on a grassy pathway along the edge of everything, along the edge of your life, walking into the quiet and laying down inside the hammock and just, resting.

Above you, trees. Cedar. Swaying, swishing, gentle. And you too in the hammock, swaying, swishing, gentle.

Just take a moment.

Hush.

Do you know what you want yet? Do you know how to get it? Or do you actually want nothing but this. The swaying. Because that is fine. Everything is fine here in Ewok Village. That's how it is. Nothing needed.

Rest.

Allow rest to actually come to rest in your body. Allow it to root. Water it. Watch the rest grow and let it overgrow you as you let yourself to return to nature, like a building left alone. Let rest become you, and I will tell you the story of Ewok Village, the story that I am already telling you.

○

Ewok Village is a clearing in the woods on the outskirts of the crops next to Malo's corn, separated from everything by thick trees and a grassy pathway that goes along the farm perimeter.

At Ewok Village, there's a mossy log, a wooden pallet, and a pink woven hammock that we ceremoniously hang in May 2013 with a six-pack of beers one of our first weeks living all together on the property — Matthew, Alex, and I.

I am having one of the best and worst summers of my life. It is busy and fast, hot and confusing, yet also slow and filled with moments of quiet reflection, many of which happen here at Ewok Village.

Ewok Village is Matthew's idea. Matthew is the farm manager who just came off the Pacific Coast Trail with his dog Trout, the best dog I believe any of us have ever known with shiny apricot hair and a medium build; a retriever mix, and a smile for days/weeks/a cosmic eternity immeasurable as his goodness as he lays around in the oats and runs alongside Matthew, who seems to equally imbue a certain kind of magic onto everything around him. The two of them live in a small 2-bedroom house on the property that we meet outside of every morning to plan our day in the carport/clearing house for all the produce that we harvest and where we always listen to KPIG radio out of Freedom, California and begin the day with a Wendell Berry poem.

Matthew is one of those people who has a very specific personal mythology like this — things that he holds sacred, like KPIG, Wendell Berry, Trout, and ethically sourced meat. He cures sausages in the window of his kitchen, has a bow for hunting deer, and almost always has stew brewing in an old Crock-Pot.

My roommate Alex and I, farm stewards, live just down the bend of the grassy dirt road from Matthew, Trout, their cured meats and eerie magic 8-ball. Our home, the former staff quarters, is a big half A-frame with high sloping ceilings, two cavernous bedrooms, a living room, a funny old pantry that our coworker Micah sleeps in once a week the night before harvest days, and a small kitchen where for the entire summer I leave the jazz radio station playing day and night.

Red Barn Ranch where we call home for this time is a rundown former summer camp that was opened by Elgin Baylor, a basketball star from the 1960s Lakers who created it for inner city youth to experience farm life and basketball on an old court now surrounded by blackberry bushes out on the way to the beehives.

Outside of our house is an old bathhouse next to a filled-in swimming pool. Behind it is Larissa's house. She manages the kids' horse camp run out of the same piece of land. Between us and Matthew is a gymnasium. And right beside us is an ancient

55

dormitory where we occasionally have to go to reset our wireless router.

I describe the place to my friends as the setting for a Goosebumps novel about a haunted old summer camp.

The dormitory is especially spooky. The first time Alex takes me in there, I notice the windows to the bathrooms are ominously painted red and the rooms are packed with things like egg foam mattresses and vintage roller skate boxes. Thinking we are alone, we hear strange noises and accidentally surprise two teenage boys who work for the horse camp playing video games in this dark spooky dorm where they've apparently taken up residence. How they kept themselves secret living in a building 10 feet from us I still have no idea.

◯

Ewok Village is where I go when I am alone, but not. It's where I go when I'm on the threshold of my life. It's where I am heartsick, confused, falling both in and out of love, all while laying in my therapist's office, which is this fading pink hammock in the woods. It's where I feel ashamed for pursuing a new life, for wanting it at all, and where at the same time I embrace the notion of being changeable. It's where I try to forgive myself for being happy in a new and different way. Where I mourn the happiness I had before and have foregone. It's where I make a playlist called "pocket jams in the woods." And it's here that I make the step toward trying to live in a way that makes sense now rather than before. That's what it is here. The forest is the only place I've ever felt able to be this fragile. This kind of forest I mean, the parts of it that for some reason feel more warm and personified than others, like the trees could start talking and it wouldn't be all that surprising.

In many ways Ewok Village is a place in the mind as much as it is anything else. Everyone deserves an Ewok Village, even if it's only in the mind. A place to go between things; language and silence, work and play, balance and unraveling, strength and weakness, ego and id, love and loss, action and rest.

○

What needs to be said when there is so much that could be? What I will say is this: summer is most summer when you don't realize it. When you are in the thick soup of it, in the deep summer that feels endless. It's only when you look back and realize that it isn't endless, exactly, that you say one of those old folks things like, you only get so many summers. There's wisdom in this but also the blues in the way that so many things are fleeting, the great majority of things really, and therefore almost no thing is for sure, nor is it endless. Perhaps this is why my ultimate dream is to walk through an endless orange grove, where you can't see the orange trees ending in any direction. Perhaps that is why it's hard to revisit this summer, because as deep as it got, even it ended and turned to a fall where I jogged quietly along the farm path we built the deer fence along before the rains started, and then when they did start, holed up in my big room at the tiny roll-top desk and still drove back and forth down the winding road to Seattle, just in a less hot and less fast way, not knowing where the future was headed, only that it was there appearing one frame at a time in front of me.

Psychic Soup
by Lynette G. Esposito

It has mushrooms.

Bios

Susan P. Blevins
Susan P. Blevins, an ex-pat Brit, lived in Italy for twenty-six years, traveled the world extensively, and has now settled in Houston, Texas, where she is enjoying writing stories and poems based on her travels and adventures. She had a weekly column on food in a European newspaper while living in Rome, and has published various articles on gardens and gardening while living in northern New Mexico, before moving to Houston. Since living in Houston she has been published in various literary magazines, both in hard copy and online. Her passions are classical music, gardening, nature, animals (cats in particular), reading and of course, writing. She has written a journal since she was about nine. She is a true bibliophile and has books in every room of her house.

Roger Camp
Roger Camp is the author of three photography books including the award winning Butterflies in Flight, Thames & Hudson, 2002. His documentary photography has been awarded the prestigious Leica Medal of Excellence. His work has appeared in numerous journals including The New England Review, North American Review and the New York Quarterly. Represented by the Robin Rice Gallery, NYC, more of his work may be seen on Luminous-Lint.com.

Salena Casha
Salena Casha's work has appeared in over 100 publications in the last decade. Her most recent work can be found on HAD, Wrong Turn Lit and The Colored Lens. She survives New England winters on good beer and black coffee. Subscribe to her substack at salenacasha.substack.com

Mickey Collins
Mickey ~~rights wrongs~~. Mickey ~~wrongs rites~~. Mickey writes words, sometimes wrong words but he tries to get it write.

John Davis
John Davis is the author of Gigs, Guard the Dead and The Reservist. His work has appeared recently in DMQ Review, Iron Horse Literary Review and Terrain.org. He lives on an island in the Salish Sea and performs in several bands. A poem of mine appeared in your magazine a few years ago.

Emily
Emily is a writer living in Maine, fascinated by the natural and the supernatural. She studied creative writing at UMaine Farmington where she was honored to work with Beloit Poetry Journal and be granted an Excellence in Poetry award. In Seattle, she co-created the poetry journal HOARSE which was shortlisted for a Stranger Genius Award. She is a long-time writer and editor, and also practices nutrition, hypnotherapy, and herbal medicine. She embraces herself as queer and lives with her sweetheart and their daughter who asks compelling questions like, do butterflies sit in chairs to eat lunch? Most recently, her work appears or is forthcoming in Anodyne Magazine, the Champagne Room, and Mutha Magazine.

Lynette Esposito
Lynette G. Esposito, MA Rutgers, has been published in *Poetry Quarterly*, *North of Oxford*, *Twin Decades*, *Remembered Arts*, *Reader's Digest*, *US1*, and others. She was married to Attilio Esposito and lives with eight rescued muses in Southern New Jersey.

Robert Eversmann
Robert Eversmann works for *Deep Overstock*.

Frank Gallivan
Frank Gallivan is a gay/queer Buddhist poet raised, to his surprise, in Greenville, SC. After trying on various careers, he's settled on writer/consultant/wanderer. Frank has lived in San Francisco, London, Rio de Janeiro, and a van somewhere in the US. He writes poetry to rediscover home.

Heather Hambley
Heather is a Latin teacher turned translator. She has a BA in Classics from Reed College, where she developed a passion for prose composition and mythological women. She lives in Central Oregon with her husband Andy and their senior poodle Mo. She loves watching scary movies and curates feel-good horror sets at happyspookies.substack.com.

Alina Kroll
Alina Kroll is an Oregon-based writer and editor. Her works are typically defined by deeply introspective narrators who are occasionally drawn towards the morbid or unsettling circumstances that surround their lives. Kroll is particularly interested in making unusual experiences feel familiar by creating characters who, although strange, also feel vivid and believable. You can find several of her published works in Prism.

Joan Mazza

Joan Mazza has worked as a medical microbiologist, psychotherapist, and taught workshops on understanding dreams and nightmares. She is the author of six self-help psychology books, including *Dreaming Your Real Self*. Her poetry has appeared in *Atlanta Review*, *The Comstock Review*, *Prairie Schooner*, *Slant*, *Poet Lore*, and *The Nation*. She lives in rural central Virginia.

Janet McCann

I am an ancient poet who taught at TAMU for 47 years, am now Professor Emerita. And I have done volunteer work in a library.

Karla Linn Merrifield

Karla Linn Merrifield, a nine-time Pushcart-Prize nominee and National Park Artist-in-Residence, has had 1000+ poems appear in dozens of journals and anthologies. She has 15 books to her credit. Following her 2018 *Psyche's Scroll* (Poetry Box Select) is the 2019 full-length book *Athabaskan Fractal: Poems of the Far North* from Cirque Press. Her newest poetry collection is *My Body the Guitar*, inspired by famous guitarists and their guitars, and published in January 2022 by Before Your Quiet Eyes Publications Holograph Series. Her *Godwit: Poems of Canada* (FootHills Publishing) received the Eiseman Award for Poetry. She is a frequent contributor to *The Songs of Eretz Poetry Review*, and assistant editor and poetry book reviewer emerita for *The Centrifugal Eye*. Web site: www.karlalinnmerrifield.org/; blog at karlalinnmerrifield.wordpress.com/; Tweet @LinnMerrifiel; Instagram: karlalinnm; Facebook: www.facebook.com/karlalinn.merrifield.

Timothy Arliss OBrien

Timothy Arliss OBrien (he/they) is an interdisciplinary artist in music composition, writing, and visual art. He has premiered music from opera to film scores to electronic ambient projects. He has published several books of poetry, (*The Queer Revolt*, *The Art of Learning to Fly*, & *Happy LGBTQ Wrath Month*), and is a poetry editor for *Deep Overstock*, a judge for Reedsy Prompts, and a poetry reader for *Okay Donkey*. He also founded the podcast & small press publishing house, The Poet Heroic, and the digital magic space The Healers Coven. He also showcases his psychedelic makeup skills as the phenomenal drag queen Tabitha Acidz.
Check out more at his website: www.timothyarlissobrien.com

Diana Raab

Diana Raab, MFA, PhD, is a memoirist, poet, speaker, and award-winning author of fourteen books of poetry and nonfiction. Her writings have been published and anthologized worldwide. Her latest book is HUMMINGBIRD: MESSAGES FROM MY ANCESTORS. (Modern History Press, January 2024). She writes for Psychology Today, The Wisdom Daily, and Thrive Global and is a guest writer for many others. Visit her at: dianaraab.com.

Elizabeth (Betty) Reed
I am a writer, traveler and musician. I try to write the music of life in words. My essays have been published in The Boston Globe Magazine, The Rumpus, Parents, Fifty Give or Take and other journals.

Jihye Shin
Jihye Shin is a Korean-American poet and bookseller based in Florida.

Julian T Stites
I am a local Portland OR author and caregiver. I have been an avid reader and collector of books my whole life. I am a writer of songs and poetry and I enjoy working on my novel. I live in Portland with my husband and our three pets, Nightmare, Momma and Tobi.

Marianne Taylor
Marianne Taylor is a bookseller at Powell's on Burnside where she manages the sales floor in the Blue, Gold, and Green rooms. In a previous life she taught literature and creative writing at a Midwestern college, and her poetry has been published widely in national journals and anthologies. She once served as Poet Laureate of her former small town, but for the past three years she's been trying to find her way around Portland.

Colette Tennant
Colette Tennant has three books of poetry: Commotion of Wings, Eden and After, and Sweet Gothic, just published. Her book, Religion in The Handmaid's Tale: a Brief Guide, was published in 2019 to coincide with Atwood's publication of The Testaments. Her poems have won various awards and have been nominated for Pushcart Prizes along with being published in various journals, including Prairie Schooner, Rattle, Southern Poetry Review, and Poetry Ireland Review. Colette is an English and Humanities Professor who has also taught art in Great Britain, Germany, and Italy.

Rachel Turney
Rachel Turney is an educator and teacher trainer. Her photography appears (or is in press) in By the Beach, San Antonio Review, Writers Resist, The Salt, Noom, San Antonio Review, Umbrella Factory Magazine, and Ink in Thirds Magazine.
Blog: turneytalks.wordpress.com Instagram: @turneytalks

Z.B. Wagman
Z.B. Wagman is an editor for the *Deep Overstock Literary Journal* and a co-host of the Deep Overstock Fiction podcast. When not writing or editing he can be found behind the desk at the Beaverton City Library, where he finds much inspiration.

Nicholas Yandell
Nicholas Yandell is a composer, who sometimes creates with words instead of sound. In those cases, he usually ends up with fiction and occasionally poetry. He also paints and draws, and often all these activities become combined, because they're really not all that different from each other, and it's all just art right?

When not working on creative projects, Nick works as a bookseller at Powell's Books in Portland, Oregon, where he enjoys being surrounded by a wealth of knowledge, as well as working and interacting with creatively stimulating people. He has a website where he displays his creations; it's nicholasyandell.com. Check it out!

All rights to the works contained in this journal belong to their respective authors. Any ideas or beliefs presented by these authors do not necessarily reflect the ideas or beliefs held by Deep Overstock's *editors.*